A Compilation of POEMS

Life is gift from Above, Maximize it

REV. DR. NANA ABEKA JOHNSON

authorHOUSE®

AuthorHouse™
1663 Liberty Drive
Bloomington, IN 47403
www.authorhouse.com
Phone: 1 (800) 839-8640

Published by AuthorHouse 03/20/2020

ISBN: 978-1-7283-5179-7 (sc)

Contents

Introduction

I wrote these poems out my personal life, challenges, experience and reflections. It covers basically what life means to me, my daily challenges and how to master courage to conquer them.

My personal love poems I wrote to my wife in my early days of marriage life.

My black experience in America and the challenges of black communities in a racist world.

America experience of 9/11

And my faith in God. Hope u enjoy them.

Acknowledgment

Dedicated to wife, Ewurama Johnson my mother, Faustian Baiden (passed away) two-sons Fiifi Johnson & Adom Johnson and two daughters Nyame Johnson who did my book cover & Nhyira Johnson and all loves ones. Thanks to Author House editorial team for their good work.

Hope you be inspired as read these poems.

Introduction

These poems cover a period of time of twenty years of my living in the USA and New York . It covers various topic from current events, to the Falling down of Twine Towers. Police brutality, killing of black unarmed men in New York, racial profiling and economic inequality . The death of young soldiers in Foreign land, the return of our wounded soldiers needing help and aid to survival from war in Iraq.

The struggle for minorities as to what is the true meaning of our freedom. Why our black young men are lock up behind bars.

The cry for justice and truth in our court systems.

The Comfort of love and true meaning of love.

Why love hurt sometimes and wonder of true love. The determination to rise again if you fall. The power of cruel ambition. Our determination to revenge our enemies after 9/11 to capture the enemy and it's consequences, we shall bear.

I cover various topics as listed below . I wrote 100 Poems in this book.

Hope you will be motivated and inspired by them.

Life Is A Gift from God

I am thankful to God for the gift of life.
I am grateful to God for my existence.
I am thankful for each day
As I hear the birds sing,
As I see the sun rise and set.
I am thankful to God for the gift of life.
I am here for a reason;
I am here for just a season.
I am like a flowers that blossom in summer
And fall away in winter.
So, Lord, help me and guide me
To make the right choices
and best decisions each day.
Let me not fall.
Let me not fail to achieve my purpose, and
Let me realize the reason I was born.
Help me each day to do what I ought to do,
To master courage and faith to fight my battles
And to overcome many challenges of life.
Though life might not be easy,
However, you promised to be there with me to help me.
But, if for any reason I falter, give me the grace
and strength to rise up again.
The Holy Book says that, if the righteous fall
seven times, he will rise again[1],
So give me the grace to accept my weaknesses,
Knowing that I'm human and am not perfect.
But, oh Lord, give me the strength to overcome them.
Help me each day to cultivate the right habits.
Help me to do the right thing at all times.
Give me the wisdom to discern between right and wrong,

---

[1] Proverbs 24:16

And give me the courage to choose the right path,
Though the right path may be hard and tedious.
Help me to not back off and
not to choose the easy path that leads to nothingness.
Help me not give in to lustful desire that seeks to destroy my soul,
Or instant gratification
And earthly pleasures or youthful lust.
Let not the enemy of my soul
deceive me to lose my eternal values and
eternal perspective.
Deliver me each day from temptations
And preserve my soul for your kingdom.
Direct my steps to your will and purpose each day.
Give me wisdom and grace to live to fulfill my
purpose and achieve my destiny.
As King David said,
"Teach us to number our days, that we may gain a heart of wisdom." [2]
King Solomon said,

"Wisdom is the principal thing; therefore get wisdom:
and with all thy getting get understanding."[3]

[2] Psalm 90:12 KJV
[3] Proverbs 4:7 KJV

Life Is a Miracle

It's a miracle to be alive each day.
It's a miracle to see the sun rise and shine again,
To feel the gentle breeze,
To hear the sound of music,
And feel my heart beat.
I thank God for the gift of life,
To hear the voice of my beloved ones.
To be alive each day is a blessing.
As I enjoy the blessing God has given me,
I hate to see the struggle and the pain and the burden of each day.
I am grateful to God
For giving me the strength and the grace to be alive,
To work hard to fulfill my dreams,
To smile and laugh again,
To live again and to experience life in its fullness.
"Many are the plans in a person's heart, but it
is the Lord's purpose that prevails."[4]
So I commit all my plans and aspirations,
hopes, and dreams into your hands
And ask you, Lord, to guide and lead me.
As the holy Bible says, "Commit your works to the Lord,

And your plans will be established."[5]

[4] Proverbs 19:21 NIV
[5] Proverbs 16:3 NAS

Life Is a Journey

As soon as I was born, I began this journey with life.
I have travelled long distances by the grace of God.
I have seen many faces, experienced many things.
I have travelled through many countries,
Gone to many places, seen many faces,
Met many people, rich and poor,
Some happy and some sad,
Some white and some black,
Some racist with ugly attitudes,
Some nice with open minds.
I have travelled long distances.
It's been a weary journey, like the struggle of black people.
Our journey has not been easy;
It has been long walk to freedom.
I have seen many good days and bad days.
I have seen injustice and
A series of events for each day.
Our life's story begins at the sound of birth,
At the cry of the innocent baby,
Born with grace and mercies of God.
The days of our innocence are few,
We are born into a world of imperfection,
A world full of troubles and battles,
A world of beauty and ugliness,
A world of many surprises,
A world of many unknowns.
Yet behold the joy the baby brings to our hearts
As parents, friends, and love ones gather to celebrate.
My first child was just a joy.
The joy of being alive is incompressible.
Unsearchable blessings await us each day.
Life brings many responsibilities—

The need to discover yourself,
To unleash your potential,
And to discover who you are,
To dare to be, to believe in yourself,
To believe in your dream,
To be all that you can be.
Destiny awaits you.
Knowledge and wisdom become the tools
That help you to fulfill your dream.
Work hard each day, my beloved,
Endeavoring and daring to rise to the top,
Striving each day to be the best you can be,
Aspiring to be great in your own way.
Daily dreaming will help you to move forward.
Work hard toward achieving your dream.
Therefore, let nothing stop you.
Let no obstacle hinder you,
Cripple you from realizing your goals.
Ask God for strength and power to conquer
All difficulties and challenges.

Why Were You Born?

For this you were born,
For this reason, you live,
For this reason, you will die.
To live you must dare to dream,
To rise from obscurity to prominence.
You must dare to believe in yourself.
To live you must dare to conquer
Your inner fears and doubts and struggles.
To live you must have courage
Each day to conquer the unknown.
Have faith in God. It will enable
You to make your dream possible.
Master courage to win each day's battles.
Life is a full of many
Ups and down, twist and turns—
Good days and bad days,
Rain and sunshine,
Tears and laughter,
Sad moments and happy moments,
Lack and abundance,
Love and friendship,
Hateful enemies,
Success and failure,
With many detours.
But no matter what happens to you,
Keep believing in yourself,
You must keep trusting in God.
Ask for and seek his help at all times
To find the right path,
To ask the Holy One to help you
Make the right decisions and choices.
Keep dreaming and keep believing,

No matter the problems you face.
Keep believing you can win and make it.
Have an open mind to receive new information and ideas.
Keep learning new things each day.
Have an open heart to love.
Be humble to admit your mistakes.
Ask for help when you need it.
Keep a positive attitude; it will enable you to be better.
Do not be too proud to say sorry
when you make a mistake.
Do not be too arrogant
and proud to extend a helping hand
to some who might need your assistance.
Help others if you can.
Serve others with your gifts and talents.
Give a helping hand to someone
Who needs your help,
If you can.
By serving others you fulfill your dream,

All Days Are Not the Same

Keep hoping.
Some days are as bright as the sun.
Some days are as dark as a thousand nights.
Some days are rainy and stormy.
Some days are rough and tough and as hard as iron.
But no matter what your day or night might be like,
Keep walking through it,
Keep hopping for the best.
So, keep walking through the rain and the storms.
Keep walking even when you cannot find your way.
Never stop walking. Never stop running.
Never stop believing
Because there is light at the end of the tunnel.

God Is My Light

"The Lord is my light and my salvation—
Whom shall I fear?"[6]
In your darkest hour,
Trust God to be your light.
Believe He will be the light in your darkest hour.
Have great expectations in life.
Think great thoughts,
Imagine the impossible,
Dream big,
Believe in your dream.
In face of obstacles and difficulties,
Never give up,
Never throw in towel.
Master your fears, face each new challenge
With faith in God that you will win each battle.
Believe in yourself and believe in your dream,
Believe that "Everything is possible for one who believes."[7]
If yourself can believe, you do it.
If you can see it by faith,
If you can dream it by faith,
Then you can achieve it by faith.
Believe in the power of the possibility through the invisible power of God.
Miracles do happen.
Seek divine assistance
each day through prayer.
Ask for wisdom to implement
Divine strategic plans to achieve your goals.
God will willingly rescue you from all your troubles.
"Many are the afflictions of the righteous,

---

6 Psalm 27:1 NIV
7 Mark 9:23 NIV

But the Lord delivers him out of them all."[8]
May the Lord deliver you from fear of the unknown.
May His face shine on you;
May he give you peace.
May the Lord guide you with His eyes,
And may His spirits lead you each day.
Stay strong. Fight on.
Never give up on your dreams,
Because dreams come true.
Have hope in times of despair.
Never panic in the face of adversities.
Never give up.
Stay strong and fight on.
Victory is sure to come if you persist in the name of the Lord.
Have faith in God. Keep believing.
God answers prayers.
Prayer moves mountains and changes things.
So never give up.
And in the face of great obstacles
And insurmountable mountains,
Do not throw your hands up in despair.
Hold on firmly to God.
His hand is unfailing in times of despair.
Trouble never lasts forever.
So, never give up.
Life is lonely path.
You have to choose your path.
You have choose each day what to do.
Where to live? Where to go?
Whom to live with?
Whom to associate with?
Life is big choice,
Yet you must make the best out all that comes to you.
Yet you must continue,
Knowing God is on your side to help you.

---

[8] Psalm 34:19

He will give you strength
and power to win each battle.
Once I travelled far from home
To a far country to make a living.
I left all loved ones behind,
As I want to an unknown land.
All my dear ones were far away.
It was a long journey,
Many miles from home.
I had to learn to survive,
To have courage to live each day.
I had to learn to survive adversities.
Faith became a necessary for my survival
And to overcome many challenges.
There is no progress without a struggle.
I dared to win my battles;
I dared to believe in possibilities.
I had to find hope
to conquer each day's battles and challenges.
But I survived
In an unfamiliar land.
I expected the best each day.
To fulfill my dreams,
I worked hard and tirelessly.
I set achievable goals.
I believed.
In spite of all my difficulties and limitations,
I believed.
I went though many rough times,
But I survived.
I believed in God
and trusted in His divine power
To help me. And He did.
I asked Him to guide me daily,
And He did.
I have come this far by faith,

So I advise you, never give up.
Keep your hopes high. Keep working and
walking toward achieving your goals.
Be strong. Be courageous.
Be tough and brave
Because life can be tough.
Life is not fair either.
You must have a big heart.
You must be smart, courageous,
bold, determined, strong minded,
Unshakable, unmovable, purposeful,
Single minded, well focused—like a rock.
Do not be feeble minded.
Stay strong and
Play by the rules.
There are no easy answers.
There are no shortcuts.

Never Give Up

Never give up your hopes in life.
Never give up your dreams in life.
No matter how tough things might be,
Never give up your faith in God.
He will see you through all your difficulties.
He will give you grace and strength if you ask Him to help you.
Never give up if you want to win.
Do not give up, no matter how dark the night be,
Because the sun will shine tomorrow.
So keep the faith.
Keep believing.
Things will get better.
They may get worse before they get better,
But that's okay. Accept the challenges.
Men like David teach us
We can rise if we believe.
You can make it through your darkest fear.
No matter what life throws at you,
in good times,
in bad times,
sad or happy,
in good health or in sickness.
Keep believing,
Keep hoping, and
Keep looking for the best in life.
Keep praying.
The Lord will help you.
If you rise,
if you fail,
You can rise again
if you believe.
Believe the sun will

rise tomorrow.
It may be dark now as thousand nights,
but the sun will rise again tomorrow.
So never give up your hope and faith in God.
Keep your hope alive.

Enjoy Life

Enjoy each day,
The blessings God offers you.
Be thankful for the blessing you receive,
Either big or small,
Either in good times or bad times.
Be grateful.
His grace and mercies will keep you.
Enjoy the sunshine,
Enjoy your life with the loves in your life.
Work hard each day,
Enjoy the blessings
God gives you each day.
Celebrate each day with loved ones.
Enjoy each moment of the day.
Enjoy your life in every way possible with loved ones.
Have fun by
Walking through the rain,
Admiring the beauty of the roses,
Feeling the gentle breeze of the sea,
Admiring the beauty in nature,
Seeing the good side in everything you do.
Don't stress yourself too much about things you cannot change,
Neither worry too much about anything,
About the unknown.
Focus on today's duties and responsibilities;
Leave tomorrow's issues alone.
Trust God to give you the wisdom and knowledge
To handle troubles when the time comes.
Accept difficult times with God's grace.
Ask for the wisdom of God to cope with them.
Enjoy whatever God has given you with humility of mind.
Enjoy your daily walk with God through daily devotion

And commitment to the services of God.
Be positive and optimistic in life.
Look at the bright side of life.
Never be pessimistic.
Don't complain too much about your challenges,
No matter how big or small your challenges might be.
Just face them with faith and hope and conquer them.
Rather, give thanks for everything that is the gift of life.

Life Is a Battle to Win

You must win your battles in life.
Life sometime is a continuous raging battle.
So learn to fight on and conquer by faith.
Be strong in faith and stand firm.
Fight the enemy like a hungry lion devours its prey,
As a good soldier fights in battle.
Never run from your opponent
Or turn your back to the enemy.
Face adversities and opposition.
Face the enemies in life,
Both physical and spiritual opposition.
Always be ready to declare war on your enemy.
Fight with every breath you can.
Master courage and faith at all times.
Defend the truth and stand for your faith,
Daringly and courageously as you win daily challenges.
Smile at life for God's grace to enable you
To courageously face life's difficulties.
Dare to be as brave and bold as a lion.
Be hungry and roar like a lion;
Fight desperately like a wounded lion.
Go after your goal and your dream
like a lion hungry to devour its prey.
Dare to conquer all your fears,
Master your doubts.
Have courage to face each opposition.
Dare to stand alone if it becomes necessary.
Dare daily, working hard to be great
By achieving your daily goals.
Aspire to do your best each day
And realize your success depends solely on your personal efforts,
Daily perspire and work continuously till your duty is done,

Completed, your purpose achieved.
Do whatever it takes legally, mentally, and emotionally to be committed.
Never doubt your ability to win.
Never doubt your potential to succeed.
Dare to believe in yourself.
Believe in God as your source of all your creativity.
Believe you can make it in spite of all your limitations.
Be inspired by your dream.
Aspire to do your best to be great.
Work hard toward achieving your goals.
See possibilities.
Envision your success.
Acquire all the knowledge you need
Work hard each day through thick and thin.

You Are Special

God made you special.
God made you unique and special.
He made you different from all others.
He gave you special potentials and abilities.
Follow his will and plan,
Follow his purpose.
It will require faith and courage,
So dare to standout differently,
To accomplish your goals and dreams in life.
There will come some difficulties times,
New challenges each day.
But master courage to face them.
Courage help you to win each battle
and conquer your challenges.
There will be some opposition by the enemy,
Some obstacles along the way.
Difficult times and situations will arise.
But never be discouraged; consider them as part of life.
There is always friction when you try to climb up hill.
Stand firm and strong,
Be bold and courageous.
Never be a coward because cowards die too early in life.
Never be afraid of adversities,
Or run away from pain, because these help you to grow.
Fight on the good fight of faith,
Fight your doubts and fears,
Before they master you.
Till you win,
Never give up hope.
Believe in your dreams at all time,
Even when gaining them seems impossible and difficult.
Do not abort them or cast them away.

When you are down to zero,
When you mess up so badly,
When you miss your target so narrowly,
Whenever your situation is so low you don't
seem to see your way through,
still keep believing in yourself.
Even when no one believes in you, never give up on yourself.
Whenever you fall flat on your face, it's human error.
Forgive yourself.
Resolve to do better another time.
Try as much as you can to get up
and dust yourself off.
Smile at yourself. Don't take it too seriously.
You will make it to the top.
Keep your head up,
Keep looking up into the stars.
You shall become a star.
Look to Jesus and ask Him to give you strength for your weakness.
Ask the Holy Spirit to give you power to live successful each day
To accomplish your goals for his glory.
Do not fear or panic when things go bad,
Whenever you fail to live up to exceptions and love ones are disappointed.
Do not give up on yourself.
Promise yourself to do better next time.
Learn your lessons and do not repeat your mistakes.
Learn to trust your instincts at all times.
Above all, trust in the Lord at all times with all your heart,
No matter what happens in life.
Because life is not a straight line;
Its full of twist and turns, ups and downs.
When friendships do not work out well,
Accept it in good faith.
Never worry about things you cannot change.
Ask God for grace to cope.
David said "Though I walk through the valley of the shadow of death,

I will fear no evil"[9]
So keeping walking through your darkest hour
Because the Lord is with you and through each hard time.
No matter what life circumstances confront you,
Keep hoping and coping.
Let your faith enable you each day to survive
misfortune and pain to propel you to victory.
Stay positive, stay confident, stay on focus,
Stay faithful, stay confident,
And stay happy and stay on course.
Stay with the Lord because he is on your side.
He will see you through. So stay hopeful.
Keep believing the word of God.
Hope for better days.
Hope for change to come.
Hope for brighter and better days,
And good times to come,
And brighter skies.
Things will get better.
Cast away your doubts and fears.
The word says, "Fear not, for I am with you"[10]
To help you and see you through.
"When you pass through the waters, I will be with you …;
When you walk through fire you shall not be burned."[11]
When fear and faith collide,
when love and hate collide,
When black and white are at odds,
When reason fails,
When race and religion collide,
When men and women fail to reason
Due to race and religion and politics,
When we murder and kill each because we fail to be reasonable,
Whenever it's easier to hate than to love and forgive others their mistakes,

---

[9] Psalm 23:4 KJV
[10] Isaiah 41:10 ESV
[11] Isaiah 43:2 ESV

Remember they are human and not perfect.
Expect them to make mistakes
And ask God's grace to forgive them.
As I grew older, I learned to pray: "Lord, forgive us our mistakes
And trespasses as we forgive those who hurt us and offend us."
Because as human beings,
We live an in imperfect world, yet we
Live in a fallen world,
A world full of distortion,
A world full of deception.
Learn to forgive human errors and mistakes
And weakness.
Believe in God to help you.
In a world full of falsehood, how do you cope?
Be careful in your choices each day
As you walk in a world full of pain and hurts.
Walk in faith each day.
Walk steadily and confidently.
Walk through rain.
Take hold of your life and be in charge.
Hold on firmly and tightly.
Do not stumble or fall.
Your Maker will be kind to you
When you find yourself in the midst of horrible
storms of life.
Let not fear and anxieties cripple your faith.
Jesus said "Peace, be still"[12]
Once the Master Lord was with his disciples
And they were in the storm on the sea. They woke him up.
In the hour of pain and despair,
never give up.
Be hopeful.
Know what life may dish out to you.
No matter what your fate might be,
Dare to survive adversities,
Dare to take reasonable risks.

---

[12] Mark 4:39 KJV

Discover Your Uniqueness.

Have great aspirations.
Endeavor to forget yesterday's failures.
Enjoy today's successes.
Envision tomorrow's promises.
Be more determined to fulfill your destiny.
Walk in faith.
There may be mountains in your way.
With determination, cross every river.
With hope, climb every valley.
Enjoy nature and admire life.
With courage, dare to face the uncertainties of life.
With faith, conquer your fears
And rise above your disappointments.
Master your fears.

Life Is an Adventure

Life is a gift from above,
So be thankful for it each day.
Be grateful for the opportunities God gives you.
Maximize your potential;
Live fully and maximize your potential daily.
Life is an adventure,
So dare to venture into the unknown.
Step out each day in faith.
Believe in the future.
Life is a process of change.
Hope for good things to come your way.
Have great expectations
And dare to capture and conquer each opportunity
That may come your way.
Life can be exciting if you can dream
And work hard at your goals.
Do not sit idly on the fence,
Watching and hoping someone will take care of you.
Perform your duties and take care of your responsibilities.
Rather take your destiny into your own hands and do your best
To win the game.
You must win the game.
You must be in the game
And play your part and give it your best shot.
Life is an adventure into the unknown.
Never be idle. Dare to face life's challenges.
Work hard, for hard work pays off.
Success is earned through hard work.
Be committed to your dream,
Have a clear vision,
A define mission in life,
A divine purpose,

An unquenchable desire to win,
A determined goal to achieve during your lifetime.
Be stable and have firm purpose.
Be unshakable in your faith in God.
Make sacrifices to fulfill your goals.
Work hard each day.
God will eventually crown your efforts with success.
Stay focused in difficult times,
Stay positive in rough times,
Stay committed when you are
Faced with difficult challenges.
Dare to achieve the impossible.
Break your limitations.
Rise above your fears.
Conquer your doubts.
Do not settle for the ordinary things in life
or live in mediocrity.
Do not live among the common
or accept the ordinary.
Master the courage to fight on.
Dare to climb the social ladder.
Believe in God and in yourself. Dare to do the impossible.
Have faith in God. Believe in your potential.
Live fully and fulfill your purpose.
Admire the beauty of life.

Life Is a Circle of Change

Life is a circle of change.
Summer comes and
nature is beautiful.
The sun rises and sets each day,
The birds appear and sing in the early morning,
The roses blossom,
The flowers flourish in the garden,
The grass is green and beautiful.
I love summer,
But soon I realized summer is gone.
It is getting cold.
The leaves are falling in New York.
Everything around me is changing.
It's cold, and the snow is falling.
I was born and raised in Africa,
So I love the heat.
I have lived in New York for twenty years,
But I never get used to the winter.
I wondered why all the leaves fell away in New York,
And I was puzzled the first time I saw it.
In Africa and in Florida it's not so, but here,
In autumn, all the leaves fall off the tree in the backyard.
A very unpleasant sight.
Nature sheds it leaves and prepares for change,
But change is not easy for me.
Summer into winter,
Winter changing into spring.
To live, I adapt and adjust to change.
I must accept change to survive;
Everything is not the same with time.
I keep changing because of time;
I must keep evolving, maturing.

Everything material and physical goes through changes;
So as a human, I am subject to change,
And in time, everything
Is going through a circle of change,
Except eternal values.
Refuse empty dreams.
Shallow-minded people live ordinary lives.
They accept anything presented as it is.
They never question anything in life;
They never anticipate any change.
They go through the motions of life.
They become victims of their circumstances.
They are manipulated,
exploited, and taken advantage of,
cheated and lied to.
Yet they believe everything they are told.
Naive and narrow minded.
Some say it's fate, blame others for their misfortunes,
Never accept responsibilities for failures.
They prefer to shift the blame.
The rich exploit the poor.
We in live in an unfair world.
Shed no tear for me.
It is a broken world.
It is an unequal system; evil is present everywhere.
I walk on unequal footing.
But shed no tear for me.
My knees are disjointed.
I am changing for the good.
Be kind, loving, and considerate,
You are changing, too, for good.
I love change.

Moment by Moment

Love rules our hearts.
Moment by moment, nurture love.
Turning to my garden,
I prune my rose of love.
Moment by moment, my hand keeps
Turning the soil to benefit my roses
Lest my garden of love decay,
Lest my garden of love dries up,
Lest the pest eats up my love,
To destroy my tender roses,
Lest my garden of roses fails.
Let the sunshine of love
Radiate through my darkest night.
Let the sun shine through my
Deepest fears and insecurities.
Let the sunshine of love,
Radiate through our hearts.
Let the song of love keep playing.
Let lovers keep dancing together in love.
Moment by moment, I am in love with you.

Because I Am Human

To the survival of the human race in the pursuit of love
Who am I? I am just a human.
Because I am human, I suffer
hunger and thirst.
I am human so I make mistakes
And ask for pardon.
I am human so I seek peace, not war.
I am human so I desire love, not hatred.
I am subject to time and change.
Why is there oppression of some human races?
I lament at the human condition.
Why are there illness and disease,
misfortunes, hurts, pain,
poverty, war, and conflict?
I need faith to survive,
No matter what life brings my way.
I am mortal so I decay and decompose,
But I love to live, to survive,
and to enjoy my humanness.
Let us celebrate our diversities and humanity.

Come Home, Mama

Dedicated to my beloved Mama
Mama has been gone too long.
Mama has been gone; the children are crying,
The children are hungry, the stove is cold,
The fireplace has died, the fun is no more,
There is no place to go, there is no home.
There is no one to comfort us without you.
"Mama has been gone too long," my child said to me.
I wonder why you left, my beloved.
You were the hope of the children,
You were the dream of the family,
You were the backbone of all we do.
The children keep asking many questions
to which I have no answers. I wonder why.
Come back, my dear love. It's too cold here.
Come home because there is no home
without your love, without your tender care.
There is no home without you. Come back, my love.
I promise to be good this time.
It's Mother's Day, so come home to us.
Come, let us eat, play, and have fun.

True Beauty

Beauty is a thing seldom seen.
No one sees it because no one looks;
or better still, they do not look in the right places.
Beauty is held by all.
Within the soul it lies,
Waiting to come out to the surface.
Only it can't because
Beauty is suppressed by the evils of the world.
Only love can bring beauty out.
And once seen,
Beauty never hides again.
Not even hatred can deny beauty
of its true design.
Beauty, although possessed by all,
Will only ever be truly seen by a few.
And fewer yet will ever see
one of the most beautiful sights:
The beauty held by you.

Season of Joy

The snow is falling,
The trees are white,
The hills are beautiful,
The mountains are
Buried in white snow.
The children are playing,
Excited and delighted.
What a season of joy
As we sit by the fire
To warm our cold hands
As lovers embrace to
Warm their hearts
With music to soften our hearts.
A year so soon passed away,
The birth of a Savior many celebrate.
I enjoy this season of great joy
As families gather to share love,
To renew vows, to open presents.
Many surprises, new commitments.
Have fun! It's a season of great joy.

What a Wonder is Christmas

I wondered as a child
What Christmas was.
A new toy from Mummy,
A new dress from Daddy.
Presents, music, snow, fun,
Decorations in the city.
The shoppers crowd the mall,
Everyone busy shopping.
I wondered if that was all
Christmas brings.
The joy to give.
I am stressed out, stretched out now
Over what gifts and presents to give.
I wonder at the joy of it all.
Laughter, presents, music—
It's a season of joy.
I wonder if I can have Christmas without
Too much to spend.
A Savior born.
The Savior was a free gift,
So why not have free Christmas?

Forever in Love

Forever, I am in love with you.
Forever, I will be true to love.
Forever, I will keep the dream of our love.
Forever, I will honor and protect love.
Forever, I will dance with love.
Forever, I will be there for love.
Whenever love calls, I will respond.
Whenever love needs me, I will be there.
In the rain, with love I walk home.
In the storms of life, forever love endures.
In the fire of affliction, love will survive.
In good and bad days, love will cope,
Sending flowers forever to love.
Singing love songs forever to my love.
Forever, let love glow in our hearts.
Forever, let Love live on in our hearts,
Hoping and holding on forever to love.
Forever I am in love with you, in life or death.
Forever in love with you is all I cherish.
Forever let love be mine.

Love Is the Only Color I See in You

Dedicated to my sweetheart
Whenever I look at you,
Whenever I see you,
Whenever—in our garden of roses,
By the riverside—I am alone with you,
Whenever I am in your arms,
Whenever you kiss me,
The only color I see is love.
Some see you "white" and are mad.
Some see you "black." Society labels us unequally.
But what is the color of love?
Someone answer me!
But I hear no voice.
Someone asked me once or twice,
what do we have in common?
No culture, no status, no wealth.
But I love you. Is love not enough?
Why tell me what my heart feels?
Why judge others by color, not by love?
Love is all I see and all that matters to me.
A little love will end all the wars.

Loving You is All I Dream

Dedicated to my beloved wife
Loving you every moment is all I dream.
Loving you through the rain and sunshine,
Loving you with all my heart every day,
Loving you is all life is to me.
Loving you, kissing you, holding you,
Romancing my beloved is love to me.
I am lost in my world.
My dearest one, I gave you my heart,
And I am incomplete without you.
The sun loses its radiance,
The roses fail and fall away,
The sound of music ceases,
The night is darker and meaningless
Without your love.
You are my joy and my happiness.
I found peace and priceless wealth
When I found your love.
Loving you is all I desire and look for.
Loving you is all I crave for every day.
Loving you is all I dream of every moment of my life.
Loving you is all life is to me.

Guess What Love Is

I guess, if love is a dream,
Then I always dream of you,
Wherever I go and in whatever I do.
I guess, if love is a wish,
Then I wish to love just you alone.
I guess, if love ever is true,
Then I will be true to you alone.
I guess, if love is living in a fool's paradise,
I am living there with you.
I guess, if love is just a feeling,
Is that why I have great feeling for you?
I guess, if love is ever dependable,
I will be there always for you.
I guess love is more than
words, deeds, or action could express.
It is a mystery beyond the human mind.
It's only the heart that cares to know
How deeply true love feels within.
So I guess I love you
More than you will ever know.
I am still in love with you.
Many years have passed by so soon.
Many good times and bad times gone.
Many fortunes and misfortunes
have crossed our path,
Yet, I am still in love with you.
Many changes of our fortunes,
Many joyful moments we've shared,
Some painful times, we coped.
Yet, I am still in love with you.
We survived the storms and the rain.
I am not surprised that I'm still in love with you.

Many successful moments we enjoy.
See, how love binds us by time and intimacy.
Love has brought us this far on her wings
And held us as we grow old and feeble,
Yet, true love never failed us.
True love brought us many sweet moments.
I am growing old, but I'm still in love with you.
Many sweet kisses, much sweet laughter,
And many unforgettable moments
Keep me in love with you.

I Love Dancing with You

I will dance with you all night long.
I will dance with you if you invite me,
If you respond to my love, I will dance.
I enjoy dancing with you,
I am captured by your love
I am fascinated by your footsteps.
With intelligence and a sense of humor you woo me.
I will sing for you all night long.
If the music stops, I will keep dancing with you.
I will never to lose you.
I am fascinated and enchanted by love.
So I choose to dance with you.
You are very special and unique to me.
I will follow you, track your shadow.
If the light goes out, I will look for you till I find you.
I will keep dancing with you because you
Touched my heart and won my soul.
I will keep dancing by your side.
I will keep holding your hand.
I will dance all night with you
Because I have fallen in love with you.

I See Love's Reflection Through You

Dedicated to those in the pursuit of human dignity and love
Whenever I look into your eyes,
I see love's reflection.
Whenever I touch you,
I feel the warm, and you give happiness of true love.
By you I feel my heart beat.
When I speak with you,
You express my desire and my deep thoughts.
You are the realization of my dreams and my desires.
You are my desire and the reflection of my love.
By you I understand my world better and deeper.
By you I have a better
Perception of what true love is.
I conquer the world around me.
You show me the way so I can find the true feeling of love.
By myself, I could never I find this.
You reflect my thoughts and my aspirations.
You reflect my hopes and my dreams.
You reflect all that life represents to me,
And all that love could ever mean to me.

I Stir in Wonder of Love

Whenever I hear the beats of the drums at night,
I gaze in wonder.
As children dance happily,
I stir in wonder of love.
At night as the moon appears,
As I sat by the riverside, I saw the village women carry water home
And firewood for making dinner for their love ones.
I wondered how far love has brought us.
I thought about you, what love mean to us.
As I heard the dripping of waters,
I wondered what our love will bring to us as
we spent our fortunes together.
There will be many days of laughter and happiness,
unforgettable experiences to cherish.
There will be children to raise together through years.
It will require hard work.
Working hard to accumulate wealth for ourselves,
We will spend our lives together through the pattering rain.
I observe common people rise
From obscurity into prominence by passion,
Through the hissing and howling wind.
By hard work, determination, and
Dedication greatness is earned.
Success is not an accident.
But by courage, hard work, and vision
do men and women find love and achieve greatness.
So, I gaze in wonder, as by the sweat
of their brows, success is earned.

If Ever Love Was True

If ever love was true,
You will know it.
If ever love was true,
I will feel it.
If love was true,
You will neither wonder
Nor question it.
Love must be true and faithful.
You embrace love.
Love must not become too complicated,
Too hard to understand.
I doubted it.
Did the baby ever question Mama's love?
Did the baby ever ask if Mother's love was true?
If ever love changes, you will see.
If love is true, you will feel
As the baby feels Mother's love.
So let your love forever be true.
So let love forever be faithful.
So let love forever be true to love.
Love will go where love is.
Love will live forever in our hearts.

It is Worth Loving You

It is worth all the pain and tears love brings,
It is worth all the sacrifice and demands that
Loving you brings to me each day.
It is worth the friendship and companionship,
It is worth all the drama and trauma.
It is worth the laughter and happiness
We have shared through many unforgettable years.
It is worth all the changes and challenges.
It is worth all the devotion of love.
It is worth all the dreams we cherish and share.
It is worth walking in the rain with you home.
Through our up-and-down life, we enjoy moments,
Through our good days and bad days,
Through our sunshine and dark nights,
Through staying and sticking together.
It is worth the cost, through it all.
It is worth the price for everything,
For loving you, for meeting you,
For sharing our hearts and lives together.
It is worth loving you forever in my lifetime.

It's All Because of Love

___

Dedicated to my loved one
Why am I here with you
on this Valentine's Day?
It's all because of love.
I have endured this long journey with you.
It's all because of love.
Why commit I time, effort,
And energy to keep and to hold on to love?
Through the noisome night on Valentine's
Day, I, my love, remain with you.
Through the scorching sun on Valentine's Day, I send you roses.
Wounded by the pings of woeful bullets,
Through the crackling woods of flowers,
By the ticking of the clock,
Daily waiting for you to come home,
Hearing the tinkling of church bells,
Taking us to vow at the altar,
All because of enduring love.
Through the bitter cool on Valentine's Day,
And biting winds on Valentine's Day,
See how love has carried us to this end.

Life is not the Same Without Your Love

Dedicated to my beloved one, friend and partner in life
Life is never the same
Without your love, my beloved.
Without your friendship,
Life is never the same.
Life without your love
Is like summer without sunshine,
Is like winter without snow,
Is like spring without rain,
Is like a garden without flowers,
Is like a river without water.
Your love makes all the difference.
Your love soothes my pain, anchors my soul,
Satisfies my soul, comforts my heart,
Brightens my day, cheers my heart.
Your love is as true as the gospel,
Precious as gold, priceless as water.
On Valentine's Day, what can I offer you
in appreciation? I give you my heart.
What more can I give you than all I could have.
I am grateful for finding your love and friendship.

Live in the Moment with Love

I appreciate this moment because of you,
Falling in love with you once more,
Living in the moment, dreaming of you,
Seizing the opportunity.
Behold the moment I waited for!
This is the moment of our change.
This is the moment for love,
Enjoying each other in the moment.
This is the moment for peace;
Bury the weapons of war.
Cease the fights to seek peace.
With love in our hearts,
With hope in our minds,
With faith in humanity,
This is our moment.
Let's change our world for good.
Let it not pass by or elude us.
With love, we can make
our world a better place
For all humanity and for all people.

Love Is Better This Way

Make love simple,
not complicated.
Make your words kinder, clearer,
more understandable, not too difficult.
Make love touch tenderly,
No crooked, uncertain ways.
Make love predictable,
No wondering in the night.
Show me the way carefully,
Lead me gently and tenderly.
Do not break any bone.
Be kind and peaceful.
Deal kindly with this child.
Bear tenderly and wholeheartedly.
Kiss and hold tenderly,
Gently, this way I prefer.
Love feels better this way.

Love at Home at Christmas

The season of love and care
Is once again here upon us,
So love is found at home.
Hearts are gladdened by love
From far and near.
Sweet memories of love,
Journey, and success—
Candlelight at night glows,
Lights bright on the Christmas tree,
Gifts sent from far to love.
Tender kisses and love
Shared by dear ones to stir love.
So to home I go to love.
Smiles and laughter. My heart gladdens
To cheer my desperate soul,
Hoping and expecting.
A New Year is coming once again
With new hopes and dreams.
Love is home forever to stay.

Love Is the Greatest

Love is the greatest
Of all our exploits and successes,
Of our dreams, hopes, and endeavors.
Love is the essence of our existence.
Love adds beauty to nature and all we behold,
Giving meaning to our lives,
Making the rose blossom in our eyes,
Exciting our souls with unending happiness,
Setting our souls on fire with passion,
Satisfying our sexuality with affection.
Love offers us acceptance, honor,
Appreciation, with a sense of belonging.
What is this life of ours without love?
Empty, barren, unhappy, unfulfilled.
How will this life be without love?
Boring, toiling, mourning, wailing,
Fighting. Wars and family break-ups.
Love makes all the difference,
Love is the beauty of our lives.
Love is the greatest of all.

To Love on Valentine's Day I Go

Dedicated to my true love
It's Valentine's Day I go to love,
To feast, to dance, to kiss,
To laugh with my love,
To forget some stressful moments,
To seek and to share love.
I send to my love beautiful roses.
I send to my love precious diamonds and gold.
My phone is ringing; to love I go.
My kettle is singing to make tea for my love.
Love is home, to kiss, and to keep me warm.,
I hear the slam of my door.
Love is home to kiss on Valentine's Day,
For love is sweeter than honey.
So I go to my love to share sweet love.
So I'm in love, no matter the cost.
Though it cost so much, yet I cleave for good.
To live is to love; to love is divine.
To love I commit, holding on, keeping love forever.
So, I vow to keep loving on Valentine's Day.

True Love Has No Limits

True love has no limits.
I will cross boundless oceans find you, my beloved.
I will soar endless skies to reach to you, my beloved.
True love is blind to color and race.
No, nothing can hold us bound.
I am captivated by your love.
I am move by your love.
Nothing will stop me from finding her—beloved.
True love goes beyond every distance,
Runs every race, and beats every competitor,
Wins every rivalry,
Climbs every wall, and leaps over every mountain.
With wealth and riches, he subdues her, his beloved.
Her love has survived all odds.
Enduring relationships is true love.
I hope you love me just as I am.
I hope your love is true.
I hope you accept me as I am.
I hope you stay true to me.
I have found a place in my heart for you.
Let not your love disappear
as do the morning clouds
Or melt away as early morning snow
Or leave my heart broken.
So let me know how you feel.
Deep in my heart, I am still in love with you,
But why have you so soon gone away?
Why have you left my heart broken?
I cherished you and the sound of your voice.
I cherished the moments we spent together.

How do you feel deep in your heart?
Why not be true to me
And come back, my love?
I send beautiful flowers.
We shall love again.
I truly love you, *my beloved*

True Love Sticks to the End

True love is faithful,
True love is compassionate,
True love takes time to care,
True love understands,
True love is passionate,
True love sticks no matter
The cost or coast.
True love sticks in good or
bad times, rough or tough times,
Through the storms and the rain,
Through sunshine and cloudy days,
Through lack or luck,
Through pain or gain,
Through good or ill-health,
Through suffering or soaring success,
Through fame or failing times.
Love sticks, keeps, and protects,
Cherishes, endears, and upholds life.
The beauty of human perfection,
True love offers endless devotion,
Commitment, the crown of all our efforts.
Love sticks to the end, winning our hearts.

Thanks for Your Love

Dedicated to my beloved one
I never realized I needed love
Till you showed up from nowhere.
I never thought to be loved
Till you showed me the way.
I never knew what true love was
Till you conquered my heart.
Never did I imagine that
Love is worth finding and sharing
Till you brought me roses of love,
Hope, beauty, and treasures of love.
I never thought anyone cared
Till you proved to me that you do.
Now I cannot repay you a million times.
Now I am a prisoner of love,
But forever I am grateful for finding love.
You make love awesome, a wonder.
You make love as beautiful as the roses.
You make love as precious as gold.
Thanks for sharing your love with me.
Forever will I be true to love.

May Life Be Kind to You

My Wish for My Beloved
Great Nation Mourns at 9/11

To all who lost loved ones on 9/11, and to my best friend, John.

A great nation mourns her dead.
Her enemy struck her at the heart.
Never has such a tragedy been seen;
Never has she lost so many lives.
Her pain and grief unbearable.
Evil is hateful, has struck her heart.
Yearly she relives her pain,
Remembering her loved ones,
Great, small, young and old.
Yet she finds strength and courage
To face the future and her enemy,
Hoping not to be hit once again.
So vigilant, she vows to conquer her enemy
At any cost. She handles her life with care.
She sees her life too short to play with.
Life is her gift; like a flower, it blossoms
in summer only to fade away in fall.
This is her fall—many heroes fallen on 9/11.
She vows never again, never ever again
as she mourns her loved ones yearly on 9/11.

A Nation Heals

A nation under attack
Can't afford any more pain.
A nation wounded must heal.
A nation asking questions
Must find answers.
A nation broken at heart
Must recover speedily.
No more excuses.
The price paid is
Too much to bear.
A nation grieving
Needs comfort.
A nation fears hunting,
Needs reassurance.
Broken boundaries,
Broken securities,
Broken confidence,
Broken dreams and lives.
All must heal.
In God we trust.

A Nation Calls to Unity

Dedicated to the pursuit of love and unity
A nation calls for unity.
Knowledge appeals to us to
bury our differences.
Wisdom calls us to duty.
Obligation and reason demand unity.
Our corporate purpose enforces us
To a common goal and responsibility.
Diligence awakens us to
the urgency of our time.
Great minds call for unity.
Understanding hearts consent.
Disunity weakens us,
Disloyalty is treason,
Non-patriotism is betrayal.
Over-ambition blinds us,
Self-interest separates us,
Selfishness destroys us.
So, let us unite in these hard times
For our common good and survival.

A World of False Balance

I walk on unequal feet;
I struggle to find balance,
With unequal weight,
I struggle to gain my balance.
Unequal minds struggle to comprehend an unequal world—
Unequal identities seeking equal rights.
Why not create equal opportunities
For all, no matter our beginnings.
For, after all, all people are born equal.
Who set the rules for this game?
Why unequal wealth?
Why few rich and many poor?
No more undue favors!
No more manipulation!
No more secret balloting, dishonest gain, and counts!
Let us play the game fairly
According to the rules.
But you can never tell.

Cruel Ambition

Dedicated to those who pursue truth and justice for all humanity.
Oh, cruel ambition drives on the hearts of many a dictator.
Cruel ambition rules with
Unmerciful and wicked hands.
Humanity suffers from tyranny. Oh, cruel ambition!
Making wars, creating hate fights.
People aim for and desire success at any cost,
by any means whether fair or foul.
Don't stare at me, oh, cruel ambition.
Don't send the children to an early grave.
Oh, cruel ambition, don't send them too young.
Don't make orphans and widows cry
while we wait, but our young never return home.
Let not our young die for no just cause.
Don't blind us, oh, cruel ambition,
When people can neither feel empathy, compassion,
or mercy. While humanity suffers, we die
In your hands. Oh, cruel ambition, spare us.

Dare to Be All You Can Be

Dare to dream all you can.
Dare to be all you can be.
Dare to believe in yourself.
Dare to rise from
the dust of despair.
To achieve unending and daring success,
Dare never to feel inferior.
Always smile with confidence.
Dare to believe in your possibility.
Believe in the seed of your greatness.
Dare to go beyond your limitation.
See the beauty of your success.
With passion and desire, win your battles.
Dare to embrace love and hope.
Dare to manage your pain and hurts.
Hope to change your future and see a better tomorrow.
By dreaming possibility,
Dare to pray each day.
Dare to live completely.
Dare to enjoy life in its simplicity.

Don't Kill the Truth; It Will Survive

Oh, kill me not; I am the truth.
Oh, murder me not; I am the truth.
Oh, suppress me not; I am the truth.
Why not appreciate me?
Ask for my assistance.
No matter how deeply covered,
Intelligent minds look for me
And will draw me back to life.
Honest hearts consult me in secret
And seek to speak me out.
Sincere hearts fight my cause willingly.
I, truth, expose wild tricks
And ugly lies.
I am transparent; why hide me?
I transcend time and space.
I, truth, will survive,
Living in human hearts
And consciousness,
Winning the battle of life.
I am truth, and I live on.

Dress My Wounds

Dedicated to all in the armed forces who defend the country
Who will dress my wounds?
Who will treat my pain?
Cry, wounded soldier.
Carry me home to love.
So deep and sharp is my pain.
Cry, wounded soldier.
I am hurt from fighting
For my beloved one.
I am wounded from fighting
To defend you.
Treat my wounds.
I gave you my life;
Give me your love.
I gave you my heart;
Give me care and help.
I was there for you;
Be here for me,
Thus cried the wounded soldier to his
Beloved nation.

Go Home, Soldier

The war is over.
Go home, soldier.
But suddenly a shot
Struck my partner.
He died in my hands.
Go home, soldier.
But I can't go home;
I lost my dear partner.
How tell I his loved ones?
The war is over,
But mine has just began.
I sat still in silence.
No home for me—why?
My best friend is dead.
My heart is broken; his heart not beating.
Nightmares, horrific dreams,
Disturbed mind. I am still in battle.
Why do I carry the war home?
Neither home nor sleep for me.
Go home, soldier.

Hear the Silent Cry of the Children

To peace and safety for all our children
There is a silent cry in the land.
There is silent lamentation in our hearts.
There is a wailing and a beating of our hearts.
There is a wonder in our eyes
As we cry for our lost and mourn our dead.
As we cry for our young and wonder
When the war will cease so they can come home,
Don't say I am a coward or unpatriotic.
Don't say it doesn't matter if they die.
But for what cause? But for what war?
But for whose war? And whose fault is it?
So don't say I am either a coward or unpatriotic.
Why is there no peace? Why fight an unknown enemy forever?
Why do our young die everyday?
Why are there road bombs and killings?
Why in the dead desert? Why in a hungry far-off land?
Why are we cut in between while going nowhere?
Why do widows cry? Why are our mothers wailing?
Why are children waiting? Why are fathers speechless?
As we stare into empty air,
Why we do wonder if our children ever come home?

Help in Troubled Times

Find courage to live
In troubled times
When neither hope nor friends
Care anymore.
When alone on trouble sea of life,
I hold on to the unseen
Forces of courage.
I find courage to live on,
To face life's uncertainties.
When life offers no rest,
When comfort is lost,
When trouble moments
Overshadow my mind,
My heart finds courage
In the unseen hand above me.
To survive, I pray and plead.
My faith anchors me,
My boat does not drift.
A prayer called out.
Find courage to live on.

Honor Me The Cry of an Old Soldier

Honor me for my hard work.
Before I die, my beloved,
Honor me for my sacrifice.
For you, my beloved country,
Demands the old soldier.
Lay no flowers on my casket.
No meaningless praise from friends and
Political leaders and tearless eyes.
Honor me while I have breath.
Feed me now while I am hungry.
Give me medical care while I
Need health care urgently.
Barely can I afford to buy it.
Comfort me now, my beloved.
Give me flowers on my birthday
While I live, cries the old soldier.
Recognize my efforts, my beloved.
Life is brief and short. Love me.
Offer me my due. Appreciate me while I live.
This is the cry of an old veteran to his beloved country.

How Vulnerable Are We?

*Dedicated to all United States armed forces
who continuously risk their lives for the nation*
How did the Mighty Giant sleep?
How did the Mighty Eagle
become vulnerable to other birds?
How did the Mighty Fearless Lion
fall prey to toothless barking dogs?
Wake up, Mighty Giant! Shake it off!
Why stand and stare in wonder
While your young ones die as prey?
Secure our common good; don't sleep.
Secure our hospitals, airlines, and ports.
Mighty Eagle, make us as safe as before.
Who dares challenge you to a fight?
But they did dare, though not face to face.
Why do they hide under cover at night
In tunnels and in caves to fight you?
Will you seek and capture them?
Till we become safe and secure, will there be no rest?
But how secure is human security?
Yet we shall conquer this unknown fear.
You shall make us secure and safe again.

I Bear No One Resentment

I bear no person resentment.
I bear no one grief.
I bear no one hard feelings.
I learn to survive.
I learn to live on.
I put my past behind me.
I am no prisoner of my past.
Break the psychological chains.
I am free of my enslavement.
I am free from my oppressor.
Never did I know who you are.
Your children I see.
I bear no resentment; I live on.
Life offers me a new dream,
Brings me each day a new hope,
So I keep hoping.
Heal my broken soul, my race.
Heal my broken dream, my people.
Oh, unseen power from above.

I Keep Chasing the True Meaning of My Freedom

I was born a free man, but why label me differently?
I was born free, yet I live in a cage of oppression.
Why keep killing my sons on the streets of America?
Why these assignations on the sidewalk?
Yet I vow to break loose.
I was born a free man, but why am I surrounded by racial murder?
Why are Americans killing each other in the
name of political and racial prejudice?
Why this mental enslavement?
Why should I keep chasing the wind of freedom?
Why are we dying in search of freedom and justice?
I keep on chasing the true meaning of my freedom.
Many of my children are locked up in correction
facilities in a great nation of freedom.
Americans can win this war at home.
America is plagued.
Institutional racism is killing America.
By self-defeating habits, they kill each other.
Is this the price my ancestors paid for my freedom?
I have learned to survive each day my misfortunes,
But I vow to rise above my circumstances.
We shall rise with faith in the Divine.

I Keep Running for Mama

Mama, you're my inspiration.
Mama, you're my motivation;
Mama, you're the reason
I keep running for the gold.
And I won it all for you.
You've always been there for me.
You understand me best.
You always told me
I can make it,
So I keep running for you.
See how far I've come.
I don't know where I would have been
Without you by my side,
Nurturing, encouraging,
Inspiring and affirming that I can conquer,
if I find faith in myself.
I did find faith, and I won.
I owe it all to you.
Thank you, Mama,
And thanks a millionth time.

I keep Running from the Truth

Away from the truth,
But how far could I hide?
No place, nowhere.
My conscience I can neither
Face nor deny.
So, I keep running.
Why? I can't face myself.
Why? I can't confront my fears,
So, I keep running
Into my own world,
Full of falsehood, pretense,
Fabrication, ideologies,
Philosophies, manipulation,
and rationalization.
It makes me feel better,
So, I win the war.
Why should I say I am wrong?
So I keep running.

I Keep Running in My Shadow in the Rain

As the rain keeps falling,
So I keep running after my shadow,
But as I run, it keeps up
With me, and I wonder why.
In the deep reflection
Of my past inheritance,
I keep running in the shadow of
My psychological enslavement.
I keep running in the shadow
of my illusion of freedom and equality.
A weary journey for my soul,
To the destination of nowhere.
Feeble minds accept anything,
Fickle minds bow to anything,
Liberated minds seek the truth.
Simple minds make excuses,
Never to transcend their limitation.
So I seek knowledge to liberate me
From my psychological warfare.
I wonder, why are we all not equal?
I guess the world could be run better.

I Paid for This Freedom of Mine

No price too cheap to pay for my freedom.
No price too low to pay for my freedom.
No price too small to liberate my soul
From oppression, depression, and segregation.
No price too great, I bear for my freedom.
No price too costly to pay than the price of
My freedom. I paid it all in full
With many a precious life of my ancestors.
With their blood I paid for my freedom.
No price too great than this freedom I bear.
No price too precious than this freedom many
A stranger and unknown folk enjoy today,
Knowing nothing of the suffering I bear,
Knowing nothing of the pain I endure
For this freedom I treasure. So high,
For these songs of freedom I sing every day.
Thank God I am free at last, oh beloved.
Thank God he gave me my freedom
When no man neither willed nor wished.

I Will Rise Again

I will rise above every failure.
I will rise from every despair.
Above every negative circumstance.
I refuse to be held captive by my past
Or by my misfortune and woes.
Determined, I rise daily,
Learning my lessons daily,
Accepting my responsibilities daily,
Realizing who I could be,
Rising from the dust of my despair,
From the ashes of my fears,
Breaking my chains of doubts.
By mastering courage, I will rise again,
Allowing nothing to keep me down,
defeating every adverse circumstance holding me down.
Overcoming my past failures,
I rise to explore my present potential,
Seeking new dreams and hopes endlessly.
I rise to the top. More than ever I am determined.
Ever believing, I will rise again. So I will.

I will Send a Gift to Someone Unknown

Christmas is here again. The snow has begun to fall.
I am sitting by the fire warming my hands.
My heart is wondering, asking whom I will send present to.
I have few names but a lot of money.
I guess this year for a change
I will look for a needy child.
I will go to a homeless child.
I will reach out to a needy friend.
I will send them a present. All my friends are well to do;
They do not need my present anyway.
It will not make any difference to them,
So I will look for a needy child
Who will appreciate my gift.
I will send my present to him or her.
So this Christmas, look for a
Needy child and send a gift.
Make a child smile, just for a change,
Merry Christmas. Make a child smile.

I Wonder Why Me!

Dedicated to the love for my beloved
What is this wonderful feeling?
Inexplicable, overwhelming,
Sweet, incredible, exceptional,
But heartbreaking?
When I see you, I am fascinated by your love,
Am overwhelmed by love.
I am occupied every second by thinking of you.
Every day I wait to see you,
Every night I dream about you.
I look forward to seeing you each day.
This is more than I anticipated.
Love is strange.
Why me?
I wonder,
why me?
It is strange and funny.
How do I express or deal with this?
Love can be a strange feeling. But
I am surprised you don't feel this way.
I am surprised you keep running from love.
You keep hiding from love.
I wonder why I feel this way for you.
When you don't. I wonder,
Why me?

It's Been a Long Walk to Freedom

Dedicated to the pursuit of human freedom
It's been a long walk to freedom.
Tell the children! Many never know how
we got here, so tell the children.
Let no stranger tell or write our history.
It's been many nights of tears and crying,
Many days of hunger as we prayed.
Many years of struggling, fighting, and dying,
Getting this far by the help of the Almighty.
So tell the children not to lose
sight of the value of their freedom.
So tell them never to get locked up again.
In the vanity of their imagination,
Let not their perversion lead them
To the land of no return in the pursuit
of their vain pleasures and misconduct.
Tell them it's been a long walk to freedom,
Through much toil and labor, by many tears,
Through many misfortunes, dangers, beatings.
It's been a long walk to our freedom.
Tell the children to value and preserve their freedom!

Keep Holding on For Victory

Keep holding on
No matter what happens,
No matter how low
you go down or how
horrible the darkness may be.
Wait for the appearance of a
new day in the distance.
The sun will shine on you.
Never do cut the trees
Because their leaves keep falling.
Wait for rain to come.
They will blossom again.
They will be all right; they are subject to change.
Never leap out of desperation.
Wait for the rain to arrive.
Though longer than anticipated,
It is worth the wait. It is more profitable to wait
Than to give up. Keep on
Keeping on to keep on holding on.

Keep the Faith of the Fathers

Keep the faith of the fathers.
Keep the boundaries they set,
Keep the victory they won,
Keep the dream they stood for,
Keep the values they fought for.
Honor the faith they cherish.
Make reasonable changes if necessary.
Never stray too far from them;
Never deviate from their wisdom.
Never despise or forsake the rules;
Never break the foundations.
Keep their counsel,
Follow their path,
Follow the honesty and the truth
they died for.
Always honor the fathers.
Always honor those who
stood and fought to
Make life better for us.

There Will Be a Brighter Day

After this storm is gone,
There will be sunshine tomorrow.
After this rain ceases,
So I will keep standing through
This rain till it's gone.
But this storm has been horrible,
But this rain has been destructive,
But this rain washed away all my hopes.
This storm has been painful and hurtful,
Yet I will survive this rain once more,
Yet I will survive this stormy night.
Suddenly, I realized my storm was over.
Fortunately, I made it through this storm.
Luckily, I realized my storm was over.
It's a bright summer day. My storm is over.
I have survived the storm once again.
I am a survivor. I made it through the weary night.
I made it through the horrible storm.
Thank God my storm is over.

Never Throw Away the Dream

Never abort your dream
Due to prevailing hardship.
Never cast aside your dream
For being weary of life.
Never throw away the dream
For no resources.
There is no better reason
Than determination.
Perseverance will always win,
Resistance will conquer fear,
Confidence drives you on.
Plant the seed of the dream.
Nurture and water it
With your tears
And the sweat of your brow.
Believe in the dream.
Believe in the seed.
It will grow, and you
Will be proud to dream again.

Never Take Love for Granted

Never take love for granted.
It may fly away if disappointed.
Never abuse love; it's too fragile.
Never mistreat love; it's too delicate.
Handle love with care as much as you can.
Always be tender and gentle to love.
Never break love's heart by unkind words.
Never take love for granted by neglect.
Never be too proud to honor love.
Never be too forgetful to send flowers
and presents home on love's birthdays.
Always utter kind words to love.
Always cherish love, honor love.
Always be caring and passionate to love.
Always be faithful and true to love.
Never take love for granted by any means.
Never break love's heart.
Always honor, respect,
And cherish loved ones.

A New Year Is Born with New Hope

A new year is born so soon.
Many new hopes are birthed in our hearts.
Many dreams, resolutions are envisioned.
As the old year is slowly vanishing away,
The sun is setting, to rise again on us.
The darkness is gone; new light appears.
The weary nights of the year are gone,
Wearing away, many fears buried with them.
Many new dreams now awaken in our hearts with
New strength, endless zeal, great ambitions
Born in our hearts as the new year births.
So, I keep dreaming. So, I am hoping once again.
So, I gave up many old, unwanted, and unfulfilled
Dreams as I await the new year.
So, I smile once again with a new year.
As I look to the horizon of a new year,
May it be my year of hope and greatness.
May it be your year of great achievements.
So keep dreaming and hoping for greater things.
As a new year is born once again.

No More Empty Promises

I give up empty love.
No more empty promises,
False pretense of love,
Undependable promises,
Uncommitted to love,
Except self-interest.
Why are your feet cold?
See, your heart is cold to love.
See, insensitive to feelings.
See, your hands too cold to hold.
No passion in your eyes.
Why keep breaking my heart?
Why keep following me?
Why keep sending empty gifts?
I seek no more empty love.
Enough dissatisfaction!
I drift no more.
I found faith to hold on to love.
I found true love to hold.
I found true love in your eyes.

Our World Cries for Great Leadership

Dedicated to the great leaders of our time
There are many questions
But few answers.
There are many problems
But few solutions.
There are many politicians
But few great leaders.
There are many men
But few good fathers and husbands.
There are many women
But few loving mothers and faithful wives.
Great leaders solve problems;
Great leaders create change.
Wisdom, prudence, great thinking.
Educators, philosophers,
Peace lovers—
Reason and intelligence are found in them.
Great leaders emerge in critical times.
Where are the great leaders of today?
Who dares to change our world?
Let them rise and come forth.

Our World Would Be Better Without War

When persuasion fails and
When diplomacy fails, people go to war.
When love fails, lovers fight and break up.
Yet a little compromise,
And our world will be a better place
For all the human race.
Our world would be more enjoyable
Without religious zeal
And fanatics fighting.
Our world would be safer without
Hate crimes and racism.
Our children die; elders are killed.
They are helpless and can't run.
Women cry and lament.
No comfort. Pain and hurt too deep.
Our cities are burned down,
Investments and properties lost
As we stare in wonder.
Let all religions pray for peace
and stop the fighting.

Spread Your Wings and Fly

Let nothing keep you,
Let no obstacle distract you,
Let no mountain obstruct you,
Let no misfortune break
Your wings to fly.
Let no fear of the unknown
Hold your wings bound.
Spread your wings of faith.
Fly away to your destination.
If you believe in your dream,
You will be inspired and motivated
To fly away to success.
You were made to fly,
Oh, Great Eagle, so, make the effort.
Believe in your abilities and
Talents. Find undiscovered potential.
Spread your wings and fly.
It will fascinate you
How high you can go
If you try, try, try and fly?

Steady My Course

Dedicated prayer for divine guidance and help for my soul
Steady my course, oh thou Unseen One.
Direct my way in this stormy weather.
Hold my course in this boisterous sea
As my sails meet unforeseen storms
In this trouble sea of life.
Help me to find my way, oh dear Lord,
In these unpredictable storms of life.
As I struggle through life's pathway,
Hold my course, hold my hand, my dear Lord.
Keep me from going astray and wayward.
In my misfortunes and adversities,
Hold my sails. Keep me from hitting hidden rocks.
Direct my sails safely home, precious Lord.
Let me not sink in this stormy sea of life.
Hold my sail steady home, oh Merciful One,
That I will see loved ones once again. I have long been gone.
I have long been tossed to and fro. Too long.
I need to survive to make it home, oh dear Lord,
So hold my sails, my course, and my hand, dear Lord.

Tell the Children to Come Home

Let the children come.
Gone too long from home,
Fighting and dying too young.
Implicated many times
Though innocent.
Except proven innocent by DNA,
They languish in isolation,
Blinded by color, labeled by society.
Urge them to come home.
Why not feel safe and secure at home?
Too many dangers on the streets,
Trapped too often on the streets,
Nowhere to hide; nowhere to go.
Drugs, murder, and crime—
An incurable epidemic on the streets.
Why survive on the mercy of the law?
Nowhere to hide, nowhere to go.
So, tell the children to come home.
A broken race, a broken people.
Come home. There is no place like home.

The Will to Conquer

Oh, blind ambition, lead us on
To climb greater heights
And deeper depths. Oh, blind ambition,
The will to conquer will not die.
One reason is to invade every
land and capture every foe,
Subdue every opposition,
Silence every threat and fear.
With courage and success no more than
an illusion of the mind, reason no more.
Silence the critics, oh blind ambition.
Steer people on to their fatal end.
No rule to observe; the will is to conquer.
So strong the desire for wealth; it drives
Ambitious people to their bloody course,
Ruling with no mercy, no love, no
care, only by blind ambition,
No compromise, no reason.
Blind ambition drives them on.

The Empty Night

The night is void and empty
As the silence drifts
Lingering through the cold winter.
The dreadful night dreams
Scare my feeble heart to death.
The empty night lingers long
Through the bitter, biting,
Cold winds as the night drifts
With a cold and lonely heart.
Love gone, my night is empty.
No star ever seems to appear.
No moonlight to cheer my heart.
Just an empty dark night. No love,
No sound of music, no play.
Just an empty darkness; no light.
Meaninglessness and restlessness
Overshadows as the owl flits and hoots
Through the empty night,
As love eludes my heart.
It's just an empty night.

The Inequality of Life

Some born into wealth.
Some survive poverty.
For some, life smiles to them,
For some, life is unkindly cruel.
The paradox of life.
Struggling for freedom dies.
Human error and fallibility,
Human imperfection,
All are created equal,
Pursuing the ideology.
Martin Luther King Jr. murmured,
Only honored and accepted
By death, appreciated after death.
Our world he made better,
Our world he changed.
He stood up. He spoke out for all.
So why honor him and love
Him only when he is dead,
not while alive?
Time has proved him right.

The Power of Forgiveness

To human unity, love, and peace
Oh, the wonder of forgiveness.
Humans cry for it; let it go.
Oh, the power to let go when it hurts badly.
So we hold on; it hurts too much to let go.
Why rob me of my honor, my joy, my dignity?
Why call me names I never deserved?
Why discriminate against me or classify me unjustly?
Why label me and others
unfairly while you never knew us,
Though we never met? Why wrong me?
Oh, how feeble is your nature, so you wrong me.
Why wrong me and others unjustly? I wonder why.
While in honor, power, glory, yet we all err.
Yet it's my choice now to forgive you.
So I let go, but do you deserve my forgiveness?
Though it hurts, yet I let go, but do you merit it?
So I accept your apology, but are you honest?
So I extend my forgiveness, but are you sincere?
Sure, you are a fallible human being as I am, so I let go.

The Price of a Soldier

To all who sacrificed their lives for our nation
To liberate you,
I gave up my life
So you could live in peace.
I must kill the enemy.
I keep running in the desert.
I left my loved ones at home.
If I see the sun any day,
It's my lucky day.
I live with death every moment;
I see death every day.
Comrades and enemies die around me.
Wounded partners I carry to shore.
This is the price of a brave soldier.
But I love to defend my beloved country,
Love to fight a just cause for my country.
I love to defend the truth for the innocent.
I vow to defend you, my beloved country.
This is the price for being a brave soldier.
I vow to be a brave soldier with no regrets.
I love to be a brave soldier defending you.

The Rain Washed Our Hopes Away

The rain is come and gone,
But the harvest is poor.
The rain left us nothing.
The rain brought great suffering.
We worked so hard but are now poor.
The rain took everything away.
It flooded our land, broke our homes,
Washed away our properties, our dreams,
Cherished lives, loved ones lost.
Our cats purring, our cows lowing,
Our dogs barking, our lambs bleating
For survival, but to no avail.
Listen to the murmuring streams.
Listen to the lapping water
And the pattering rain flooding,
Breaking down our homes and lives,
All our hopes washed away untimely.
Life is not fair many times.

The Road May Be Rough

The road that leads to success
Can be rough and tedious,
But stay on it if success will be yours.
The road to victory may be hard,
Full of dedication and commitment,
Buy you stay on if success will come your way.
The road to great achievement
Comes with great demands of labor and toil,
But such has been the story of all great
And successful men and women who,
While others slept, stayed awake
Burning the night candle to climb the ladder
Of success, while their fellows slept.
Muster courage, faith, and hope daily.
Muster determination, fortitude, and perseverance.
Never give up till you reach your destination.
Never look back or be discouraged.
Keep steady, focused, resolved
Till you embrace success at last.

The Rule Must Be Fair for All

Justice is the road of fairness.
Truth preserves society.
Why not seek truth at all times
And at all cost?
Why not speak the truth for all?
Why shouldn't the truth
be the standard for all?
Truth will liberate all.
Truth is the basis of the law.
Why deny the poor justice?
Shouldn't the law protect all?
Shouldn't the law be reasonable?
He who interprets the law
makes it sound good or bad.
He who enforces the law
Protects society
With pure conscience.
The rule of law must apply to all.
The rule of law must be fair to all.

The Wonder of Life

To the pursuit of truth and equality for all
Oh, look at the wonder of life!
Oh, see the beauty of life!
As a baby is born, tender, fragile,
Innocent. Oh, the wonder life
brings to us, yet pretty soon all is gone.
Oh, the joy success brings to our hearts,
Yet the labor of each day to endure, so
We bear, fears to conquer, pain to endure,
Faith to muster. Oh, the wonder of life.
Yet the pain to overcome the loss of life
And loved ones. Oh, the mystery of death.
Oh, the sight of inequality I can't bear.
Oh, the pain and horror of poverty I hate.
Oh, the wonder of misfortunes.
So I hope you bear life with gentle hands,
With care, patience, and faith.
Admire the beauty of life each day.
Enjoy each day as a gift from the Maker.
Take each day as it comes, one step,
Hoping and believing all will be well with you.

There Is No One To Love but You

On Valentine's Day, there is no one
I could ever desire more than you.
On this Valentine's Day, nothing is worth
More than loving you.
This Valentine's Day, no dream is
Greater than our friendship and love.
This Valentine's Day, there is no one
Ever I could wish for more than you.
As the crow crows and struts proudly,
On this Valentine morning,
As I awake beside you,
Nothing truly satisfies my soul,
More than your gentle voice and laughter,
Your tender touch.
In the whispering wind,
In the bubbling waters,
In the shrieking whistling,
There is no one I want to love on Valentine's Day
Except you, and to share my heart forever.

They Changed Our World

They changed our world.
Luther brought Reformation
To the church;
He dared question the
The basis of his faith.
No more endless panacea,
Self-torture to earn salvation.
Religious freedom he pursued.
King challenged social justice;
He dared challenge the great eagle
To fight, and not hurt,
So, He died for the truth.
He called great minds to reason,
He challenged our conscience,
He summoned us to question morality,
Pursued he the truth of our existence,
The purpose of our freedom,
And equality is meaningless
Unless fully practiced,
For all people are born equal.

Though Murdered, His Dream Lives On

He was our prophet,
He was our great teacher,
He was our leader.
Why murder him in cold blood?
He was our light who
Shone brightly in our
Darkest hour, yet you tried
To kill our hope.
His death made it brighter,
Better ever to shine.
His voice ever to hear
Beneath the valley, heard his voice,
Crying "All humans are born equal."
He showed us the way.
His eyes saw the Promised Land,
Though he never got there.
But we got there.
We are there today, we saw the Promised Land.
Is this all the promise is?
I wonder if it's better than before.

Time Enhances My Possibility

Believe in possibility,
Time, hence creating my chances,
Time the womb of my possibility.
Time enhances my change.
Time enhances my dream.
Time determines my manifestation.
I transcend time, space,
Evolving my possibilities.
I embrace faith and hope.
I conjure time to behold my
Victories over failure.
Time changes my fortunes.
Time changes destiny.
Time I implore and entreat.
Time yields my gains.
Time brings forth achievement.
Time, I pray, stand still
Till I conquer these fears
And win this wanted war.
But time waits not for any man.

Truth Never Dies

I, Truth, never die.
If buried, I will rise again.
If covered today,
I will appear tomorrow.
I will beat all the odds.
Never underestimate me.
Sorry if anyone rejects me.
Many great and famous I expose
and disgrace for hating me.
Don't run from me. No hiding!
I will question everyone,
I will pursue all liars,
Till I uncover them.
Many wise seek and love me,
Embrace me every day, everywhere,
All the time. I never die.
I hate injustice and oppression.
Love me and be happy.

We Celebrate You

Why kill a good man?
He was our moral teacher,
He was our inspiration,
He showed us the way
To the truth.
He fought for injustice,
Taught equality for all.
He was our leader, a prophet.
He changed our nation's heart.
He was our hope and dream.
Yet never ripe and plunged,
Plundered so soon.
He passed away from us.
Now we mourn you yearly.
Now we miss you daily.
Now your voice echoes in our hearts.
Now we love you dearly.
Now we celebrate your birth,
Treasure your achievements.
We celebrate you.

We Wouldn't Survive Long Without the Truth

Do not turn a blind eye on me.
Do not pretend you don't know
Who I am to you.
Don't try to bury me.
Don't disagree with me.
How will you survive without me?
I am your life and light,
I am your teacher from old.
I preserved you from corruption,
decay, falsehood,
and deception.
I inspired you to fight
Oppression, injustice,
Inequality, racism, and sexism.
I liberated your children.
Guess who I am?
The wise and the old listen to me
And follow my principles of life.
I am truth. You can't
Survive without me.

What is the Essence of My Existence?

Why am I here?
Where do I go from here?
I wonder if I am an atom
Existing with neither meaning
nor purpose. A meaningless sound,
A whistling wind drifting
Without any direction or destination.
I wonder if I was fashioned
By an unseen hand of a creator
Who made this world with a purpose,
Who gave me a role and a purpose.
Maybe Mama was right when she told me
There is a God somewhere who created all humans,
Who loves all humanity to live in peace.
But why is humanity in a mess?
May be there is a God somewhere
Whom I cannot see, but why am I here?
Why all the suffering? Why am I here?
May be there is a God somewhere.

When Life Becomes Unfair, Never Give Up!

Her tears seemed not to end.
Heartbroken, but never to give up,
Lost for words, lost world,
As she buried her only son.
Like a promised beautiful flower, he blossomed,
But untimely gone by death.
Life seemed not fair to her.
His graduation is this summer.
Never give up on life.
When life seems unfair,
Hope and hold on.
The sun will shine again.
Hope for a better tomorrow.
Though the night may be dark,
The sun will rise tomorrow.
Your heart, beloved, comfort,
A better tomorrow, dream always,
So she vowed to rise. No darkness.
He is gone, but she must survive.
Survive, no matter your lot in life.

Where Would I Be Without Your Love?

Dedicated to a beloved friend
Where would I be without you by my side?
How far could I go without you?
I hear your voice beside and behind me.
It's the voice of my beloved
Helping me through my stormy days,
Urging me through in my darkest hours,
Whispering words of love, hope, and faith,
Holding my hand to cross over to other side of life.
In my moments of fear,
He is there for me.
In my moment of doubts,
He speaks words of faith to my heart.
In my moments of despair,
He became my hope and anchor.
So on this Valentine's Day,
I send you dozens of roses to thank you.
How would life be without your love?
Unbearable, unpleasant, unhappy.
You brought many happy moments,
You gave me many joyful dreams,
You gave me your love, your heart, and
Your faith to lean on when I was weak.
I am grateful for your love, my beloved.
So be my Valentine today and forever.
I am grateful for finding love through you

Who Is This Stranger I am In Love With?

Who is this stranger I can't forget?
Who is this stranger
Whose voice seems familiar,
Who touched my heart
Once in my lifetime?
Who is this stranger
Who has become my dearest friend, dependable, caring,
understanding, thoughtful,
tender-hearted, compassionate—
More than I ever dreamed?
Who is this stranger who calls
With passion my name,
Whose personality I cannot
Resist falling in love with,
Who has become my best friend,
Who has brought me new dreams
and great comfort?
I guess you are that stranger.
If not, then I am undone.

Why Blame Me?

Why should the innocent suffer?
Tearless eyes do not weep for me,
Blind loyalty.
I am suffering in silence.
See these untouchable ones?
Why not question them? Why this war?
Yet the world knows the truth.
Yet who dares face it?
Judge me not, oh, honorable judge.
Why blame me? I am just a soldier
Sent to kill my unjustified enemy.
Is this not a justified war?
No war was ever justified.
No war is fought on good terms.
We had to defend ourselves
At any cost, at any place, at any time.
A man has every right to defend himself against injustices, treason.
But who dares ask why?
Why must the innocent suffer?
Why should I be a victim of dirty politics?
As a lion lives on the lives of its prey.
I do not know; I am just a soldier.
Why can't the world face the truth?
I do not meddle with dirty politics. Never!
I am a soldier on duty, protecting my country,
but I wonder why the innocent suffer.
So, why blame me for this war?

Why Choose War Over Love?

Dedicated to all leaders who seek world peace
Why choose war and not negotiate?
Why go to war and not look for peace?
Why no mediation?
War is not the solution;
Neither is killing each other.
There is a better way.
While our children are dying,
Why spend trillions on arms?
While the children suffer hunger,
While the homeless die in the cold,
While the elderly cannot affordable medication,
While college education becomes too costly,
Why war?
Knowing how deadly its effects,
While unbearable and painful our lost.
While loved ones we can't replace die.
Why choose war? Why repeat history?
With love we shall conquer,
With understanding we resolve conflicts,
With hope we look for a better world,
With patience we spare our woes,
With love our world will be safer.
Wishing, let's all live in peace and seek love.

Why Does Love Break My Heart?

Isn't love supposed to bring happiness?
Why does love turn into painful experiences
when it promises so much joy?
When it has given much hope,
When it has given many dreams,
Why is love sometimes
An illusion of my mind,
And endless search,
A hopeless dream,
An unfulfilled desire,
Giving me nightmares, sleepless nights?
It's my unfortunate experience that,
While some find true love,
True happiness, and joy,
Mine is an endless search.
Life is sometimes not fair.
So is love. So, I wonder why love
breaks my heart. So I keep wondering why.
In the silent distance, love is gone away.
I keep running after her, never to find her.
An illusion, and endless chase.

Why Kill the Children?

Dedicated to the minority killed unjustly
Why kill the children for no evil done?
Our joy turns into mourning, our hearts break.
Why kill our children because of their color?
Paid to protect us,
Yet killing us, just a pity.
Paid to watch over us,
Yet killing us, color blind.
Why kill our innocent children in the streets?
Why kill our helpless and defenseless children?
Out to have fun, but now we bury them.
Gone out but never came back home.
Our hearts too heavy and in pain;
we mourn our dead.
Hurts too much to bear or lament. Our shock is
Beyond our comprehension. Their wedding now our funeral.
Our joy taken away forever as we wonder, why us?
Why no justice in our land? Why do we suffer unjustly?
As we wonder why we can't be safe in our own land,
Shed no tears. We've wept too long seeking justice.
Comfort us no more. Haven't we endured too much?
Why no justice in the land? Why no justice anywhere?
Our hearts broken. Why no truth in the land?
Why kill the children? Why color blind?

Why Kill the Innocent?

To loved ones who died on the Virginia Tech campus
See what his hate did to our families,
On Virginia Tech Campus.
See how the innocent murdered in cold blood.
He killed to justify his hate for the rich.
Whose fault if he could not deal
with his psychological inferiority?
Why am I a victim of his hate crime?
Life is sometimes not fair to the innocent.
We held candle vigil for them.
Now we sit and cry for our loved ones,
Innocent victims of mental malfunction,
Of a sick and hateful heart.
Oh, God, heal our hearts. Oh, God, heal our pain.
Oh, God, we pray, never again
Should we suffer as this.
Oh, Lord, have mercy on our human errors.
Pardon our enemies for their insensitive hearts.
Why should the innocent suffer?

Why Murder in God's Name?

Why sometimes does religion
Breed hate and killings?
My boy asked me;
I had no answer.
His teacher told him,
Religion makes us better.
Religion teaches love, unity,
peace, faith, and mercy.
But why do some kill by religion?
He wanted to know. I told him,
Maybe it's ambition.
Cowards sometimes hide to kill.
Never do you see their real faces
And know their motivation.
But my son began to cry and said,
"But why, Daddy? But why?"
Not satisfied with my answer.
I wonder, could you explain to him
Why murder in God's name?

Why Protect Others Not Your Own?

To the fight of truth and justice for all
While we seek to protect others,
Our own are killed.
While we seek to feed others in far lands,
Our own languish in our streets.
With little to eat and wear, no place for shelter,
I do not meddle with any man's issues.
I try to take care of my own,
So I meddle not with politics.
I am just an observer, asking why,
While we seek to develop other lands,
Our children are failing in the school system,
No healthcare for millions both old and young.
I ask why our children are dying
For unknown causes. I am just an observer.
I meddle not in any man's politics, but
Just curious to know why millions are spent on war.
I lost my beloved ones, a war never called for.
I meddle not with anyone's business but my own
So why not take care of home business before others'?

Why This Baby Cries

Wonder why this baby cries?
Will neither feed nor sleep,
Nor love, nor attention help?
She cries. Mother to work gone,
Babysitter none, but sleeping.
None to care, none to comfort.
Duties call Mother to work.
Single, hard-working mother.
Daycare replaces her care.
But mother must survive.
Bills to pay. Mother to work.
Mother must survive,
But whose fault?
See what civilization offers,
See what modernization did.
Here I sit. Baby cries for love.
Mother to work, no comfort.
I know why this baby cries.

Worry No More

Leave all your cares in His hands.
Leave all your daily anxieties and worries
Into Providence's care,
Trusting His divine power
To lead and guide you,
To assist you to face the unknown.
Learn to live daily,
Hoping for a better day
To come tomorrow,
Trusting Divine Providence,
To see you through all your fears.
So I worry no more.
I learn to trust Him
To keep me through life's
Toughest hours and darkest moments.
I worry no more.
I trust in Providence's care.

You Are My Peace

In a trouble-stricken world,
You are my peace.
When life is too hard to bear,
Faith becomes my peace.
When my heart is broken,
Faith heals it.
When the storm of life rises,
I will survive.
I found peace in you.
With my hand in yours,
You hold me from falling
No matter what I go through.
Faith keeps me going.
No matter the deep darkness,
I can sleep through the night.
The broken pieces
Faith will fix.
So look above not down.
So I trust the unseen unhand
To shape my future.

You Are All I Ever Could Dream

My beloved, you are all
I ever could dream.
You are all I could ever wish for.
You are everything life could ever give
In every flower that blossoms,
In every beauty in nature,
In every breath I take,
In every step I make.
You are on my mind, and in my dreams.
You are everything there is to me.
I feel you in the sighing wind,
I see your face in every picture,
I hear your name in every sound and voice.
You are all love is and could be to me,
You are all life could ever bring to me,
You are my Valentine, my beloved.
You are my hope and my dream.
You are my gift from the Divine One,
You are my beloved, you are my world,
You are my true love, so, be mine forever.

You Are My Angel

You are my angel,
My beloved one,
You are my human angel
Sent to assist me from above.
You have always been faithful,
You have lifted me many times
By your words and deeds.
When I felt like giving up,
You held me by your hands so high.
When I felt I was losing it,
Then you did assure me to
Count on you, so I did.
I am glad to count on you.
No matter the place,
Time, or cost,
You proved trustworthy.
You've proven more than a dependable friend.
You make me feel special,
You make me conquer my world,
You are my angel.

You Are My Unseen Friend

To the invisible one who made me
No matter what came my way,
He was always there with me.
No matter what I faced in life,
He brought me through.
No matter what life seems to be,
He gave me strength to carry on.
No matter what I went through,
He always came through with me.
In my darkest hour, in the fire and waters,
He kept me alive with His divine eye.
With His hands, He protected and shielded
Me from all my fears, troubles, and pain.
You are my Unseen Friend when no one
Cares or loves or understands.
He always did. When all failed me,
I leaned on his divine grace and mercy.
I am grateful you are my constant
Friend, counselor, helper, and advocate.
He is always there, my Unseen Friend,
The Invisible One. My constant friend He has been

You Never Know Till You Try

You never know you can
Till you try, my beloved.
You never know you can do it
Till you try your lot.
Never be afraid to try
Or to make a mistake.
Keep trying even if you fail.
Keep trying till you pass
The test. Keep on trying.
Pay the price for success.
Life offers many opportunities,
So try new things. If the old
fail, try new. Never stop.
Life is offering new beginnings,
new challenges, higher heights,
Deeper depth. Find faith to try for
Unexpected victories. Anticipate
Greater success expectations, desires.
Keep trying till you win.
Keep trying till you make it.

May Life Be Kind to You

May life be good and kind to you.
May life smile at all
Your efforts with success.
May no ill and no woe befall you.
May you be in good health all the time.
May you work hard to be rich, and
may wealth be yours.
May you find true love and happiness.
May you be content with life
And dwell in safety.
May the Lord be gracious to you.
May the giver of life grant you all your heart's wishes.
Find courage to conquer fear,
Patience to bear every adversity,
Hope to live happily continuously,
Love to comfort your heart.
May life be kind to you.